TRUE OR FALSE?

- The admission price for the Thousand and One Nights millennial celebration in Morocco is over $6,000.

- Denis the Little predicted that the world would end in the year 2000.

- Denis the Little was actually seven feet tall.

- When people in Sydney, Australia, count down to midnight, New Yorkers will still have over 12 hours to get ready for their own New Year's party.

- At the stroke of midnight on December 31, 1999, all the computers in the world will explode.

Fact or fiction? Read on to find out.
Prepare yourself for the next millennium.

Books by Daniel Cohen

Hollywood Dinosaur
The Millennium

Available from ARCHWAY Paperbacks

Ghostly Tales of Love and Revenge
Ghosts of the Deep
The Ghost of Elvis and Other Celebrity Spirits
The Ghosts of War
Gus the Bear, the Flying Cat, and the Lovesick Moose
Phantom Animals
Phone Call from a Ghost: Strange Tales from Modern America
Real Ghosts
The Restless Dead: Ghostly Tales from Around the World
The World's Most Famous Ghosts

Available from MINSTREL Books

THE
MILLENNIUM

DANIEL COHEN

AN ARCHWAY PAPERBACK
Published by POCKET BOOKS
New York London Toronto Sydney Tokyo Singapore

AN ARCHWAY PAPERBACK *Original*

 An Archway Paperback published by
POCKET BOOKS, a division of Simon & Schuster Inc.
1230 Avenue of the Americas, New York, NY 10020

ISBN: 0-671-01562-1

First Archway Paperback printing January 1998

10 9 8 7 6 5 4 3 2 1

AN ARCHWAY PAPERBACK and colophon are registered trademarks of Simon & Schuster Inc.

Cover art by Paul Blumstein

Printed in the U.S.A.

IL 7+

To Maudie

CONTENTS

CONTENTS

CHAPTER 1

What Are *You* Doing
New Year's Eve?

New Year's Eve has always been a big party night.

But December 31, 1999, is going to see the biggest New Year's Eve party in history, probably the biggest party of any kind in history.

Every year we celebrate the change from one year to the next. A change of decades is an even bigger event. The change from one century to the next is considered momentous. What can one say about the change from one millennium to another?

Haul out all the superlatives you can think of and make up some new ones. This is going to be an event the likes of which the world has never experienced. There are very few people alive today who were around to celebrate the last change of centuries. There is absolutely no one around who saw the last change of millennia.

It is not just a once-in-a-lifetime event—it is a once-in-many-lifetimes event. Some people started planning early. Back in 1979 a group of American college students who may have been worried about not having a New Year's Eve date in twenty years formed the Millennium Society. The group now boasts thousands of members worldwide and has ground-floor reservations to some of the world's biggest Millennium Eve events.

So where are you going to be?

How about the Rainbow Room atop Rockefeller Center in New York City? That's always a popular New Year's Eve spot for dining and dancing. Of course it would cost you around $1,000 per person, pricey, to be sure, but a real bargain compared to some spots. Unfortunately, if you haven't made your reservations yet you're out of luck—it's been booked up for years and there's a long waiting list. The same for the Grand Ballroom at the Waldorf Astoria. One of those who made early reservations at the Waldorf is airline pilot James Hoogerwerf of Atlanta, who reserved seating for eight. He was inspired by a novel he read in which a bunch of World War II soldiers agreed to spend New Year's Eve at the Waldorf if they survived the war.

The Savoy is to London what the Waldorf is to New York—popular, expensive, and completely booked for New Year's Eve, 1999. Another tourist attraction in London will be the Millennium

Wheel, a Ferris wheel measuring five hundred feet in diameter, the fourth tallest construction in the city. It will be positioned above the Thames, parallel to the river on the south bank, opposite the Houses of Parliament. Riders on the wheel will have a thirty-mile panoramic view— if there is no fog.

For something a little warmer you might want to join the camel caravan to the Great Pyramid in Egypt, where you can celebrate the New Year being entertained by dancing Arabian horses (really!) and palm readers who will tell you what to expect in the next millennium. That will set you back $2,385 per person, not counting airfare to Egypt. But even if you could afford it, you couldn't go because that's booked up, too.

The *QE2* will be sailing from New York to Alexandria, Egypt, on December 31. You will have a chance to rub elbows with some of your famous fellow passengers like former president George Bush and Archbishop Desmond Tutu. It's a luxury cruise at a luxury price, $1,000 a day, and it's probably fully booked by now.

Try the supersonic Concorde, the world's most luxurious airplane, and zip through the time zones as the new millennium approaches. One jet will depart from New York on Christmas Eve and wind up in Hong Kong for New Year's Eve. Another will depart from New York on December 27 and wind up in Sydney, Australia, for the New Year's festivities. Ninety-six seats are available on each plane. The price? If you have to ask you probably can't afford it. But since you asked, the estimate is about $70,000 per seat.

A more affordable spot is the Holiday Inn in St. John's, Newfoundland, Canada. Normally St. John's is not a popular tourist spot in December because it's cold and dark, but it is also the first city on the North American continent to welcome the new millennium. A special celebration is planned, and rooms are going fast.

Antarctica will see the new millennium before St. John's will. In fact it will be the first landmass on earth to experience the change of millennia. It's pretty cold there, even in December, the Antarctic summer, but you can be snug and warm aboard the ship *Explorer*—the cruise will cost a mere $5,210 per person.

It's warmer in Cape Town, South Africa. You can start your evening at sunset sipping cocktails high on Table Mountain overlooking the lights of beautiful Cape Town; then you're whisked down into the city for dinner and a countdown celebration at the splendid Mount Nelson Hotel. But it will cost you $5,590 per person—more expensive than Antarctica.

A really exotic spot is the ruins of the city of Petra in Jordan. This is familiar to viewers of *Indiana Jones and the Last Crusade*. This "rose-red city half as old as time" is a perfect place to bid farewell to the past and greet the future—at $3,845 per person.

THE MILLENNIUM

By December 31, 1999, Hong Kong will already have been under the control of the Chinese communists for over two years. But they will still be charging capitalist prices. A glorious gala in Hong Kong will cost $8,590 per person, making it one of the most expensive New Year's Eves in the world. Not to be outdone, the Thousand and One Nights celebration in Morocco will set you back $6,590 each—which sounds like a lot to eat dinner in a tent, even with the fireworks and acrobats.

There will also be celebrations at the Great Wall of China, the Taj Mahal in India, Red Square in Moscow, Machu Picchu in Peru, the Acropolis in Athens, the Eiffel Tower in Paris, and a huge beach party in Colombo, Sri Lanka, on the shore of the Indian Ocean.

In some places the preparations for the big party are already under way. The Irish have sunk a giant digital clock into the murky waters of Dublin's River Liffey. The clock is counting down the seconds to the end of the millennium. When The Great Moment arrives it will erupt into fireworks.

Iceland would be an interesting choice. Plans call for the little country to be alight with a series of bonfires to greet the new millennium. Iceland at the end of December is pretty dark, so the bonfires—an ancient way of greeting the new year in that part of the world—will be very appropriate.

The Seattle Space Needle would be an impressive place to celebrate December 31, 1999, but you're too late. That was booked for a private party years ago.

Finally, the South Pacific island nation of Samoa—just this side of the international date line—will be one of the last places on earth to say goodbye to the twentieth century. The islands are making a big pitch to attract tourists.

Those are a lot of great places to party on December 31, 1999. But they are probably too far away, too expensive, or all filled up already. So where, practically speaking, can you go?

The number one New Year's Eve celebration site in the United States, and quite possibly in the entire world, is Times Square in New York City. New York is working hard to make itself what one enthusiastic city official has called "the Millennium capital of the world."

That's not just a city booster's boast. Say what you want about New York, the city knows how to throw a party. A 1997 survey in the United States found that among those who say they are planning a special trip on the millennial New Year, the overwhelming favorite destination is New York's Times Square. It's the choice of 45.8 percent of the respondents.

The Big Apple was way ahead of other popular destinations for that special eve: Las Vegas (13.2 percent), New Orleans (8.5 percent), a cruise (8.2 percent), Alaska (6.3 percent), Los Angeles (6.3

percent), Colorado (5.8 percent), Brazil (5.3 percent), Jamaica (5.2 percent), and Hawaii (5.1 percent). (Some of those surveyed had more than one choice.)

The drop of a large lighted ball from atop the Times tower in New York City has, for years, been the symbol of New Year's in the United States. Times Square itself had been in decline for decades. Huge crowds still gathered to cheer and watch the ball drop, but Times Square was no longer the showplace it had been.

However, over the past few years this world-famous area has been cleaned up and renovated, and it's going to be a whole new Times Square for the millennial celebration. How many people are going to gather to watch the ball drop and greet the new millennium in Times Square? One million? Two million? More? No one can really estimate yet. But it is almost sure to be the largest crowd to gather in a single place in America ever. The celebration will match, and perhaps surpass, the Times Square celebrations that greeted the end of World War II.

The famous lighted ball will be bigger, brighter, and more spectacular than ever. Tama Starr, president of Artkraft Strauss, the company that has been building and lowering the ball since 1908, says, "There will be more strobe lights and maybe a hologram. Lots of dazzle and flash."

New Year's in New York is so famous that city officials are worried that potential visitors will be

The millennial New Year's celebrations in New York City's Times Square are likely to surpass the gigantic Times Square celebrations that marked the end of World War II in 1945. *(AP/Wide World Photo)*

scared away. "The biggest millennium myth right now is that New York City is sold out," complained one of the tourism officials. There are still hotel rooms available within walking distance of Times Square. But if your heart is set on joining the millions to watch the ball drop live, you had better not wait much longer before making your reservations, because excitement is building.

Want something a little more intimate than rubbing shoulders with a million or two others in Times Square? How about partying in the Jacob K. Javits Convention Center in New York City, one of the largest buildings in the world. There will be cocktails, dinner, all sorts of entertainment, and a fine view of a spectacular fireworks display over the Hudson River. It will be like those famous Fourth of July fireworks displays over the Hudson, except bigger, much bigger.

There are rumors of parties in the Empire State Building and at the Statue of Liberty, but no firm plans have been made public.

Every tuxedo within five hundred miles of New York will be rented that night. Every waiter will be working; so will every cop.

But what is *really* going to make the Times Square celebration special are the gigantic outdoor television screens that will be placed around the area. These will broadcast images of the New Year's celebrations from around the world, beginning with the Fiji Islands, near the international date line, at 7 A.M. (EST) and continuing every hour for twenty-four hours. (The international date line is an imaginary line running from pole to pole. It is where the new day officially begins.)

The screens will show the celebrations at the pyramids and the Eiffel Tower and the Great Wall of China and many of the other places that have already been mentioned. They will broadcast the scene in Times Square itself when the ball drops at midnight EST, and they will show the final hour of the last day of the year 1999, on the other side of the international date line, where the broadcasts began.

In a way those TV screens may be the real story of the millennial New Year's Eve celebrations. Let's face it, no matter how many people cram into Times Square or visit the Great Pyramid or the Great Wall, most of us, most of the world, is going to experience the millennial New Year's Eve on television, either at home or at a friend's house.

Everybody all over the world will be experiencing it at the same time. Just as people in America will see some of the world's first millennial celebrations on Fiji, the people of Fiji will see the ball drop in Times Square. TV reception may be a little difficult in Antarctica, but the well-heeled celebrants aboard the *Explorer* will almost certainly have live pictures of the ball drop beamed to them by satellite—what would New Year's Eve be without it?

In recent years Times Square has been cleaned up and renovated. It will be a whole new Times Square for millennial celebrants. *(NY Convention and Visitors Bureau)*

CHAPTER 2

After the Party

There are a lot of big events scheduled for the millennial New Year's Eve. Actually, the whole year is going to be very special.

Take New York City for example. One of the most spectacular and popular events ever staged by the city is Operation Sail, or OpSail, as it is usually called. It is a gathering of tall ships—that is, large sailing ships—in New York Harbor. There have been several OpSails in the past, including one for the U.S. Bicentennial in July 1976. No one who saw the event has ever forgotten it.

For the year 2000 the city has planned the largest tall ship parade in history. Ships representing fifty nations and stretching for ten miles will fill New York Harbor for seven days from July 3–9, 2000. An anticipated fleet of thirty thousand spectator vessels, an unprecedented

Greeting the new year of 1940 at the ritzy St. Moritz Hotel in New York. *(UPI/Corbis-Bettmann)*

delegation from the U.S. Navy and U.S. Coast Guard, and an international review will join the historic ships. President Clinton is expected to attend the July 4 festivities.

Many of the tall ships will dock at other ports up and down the East Coast during the year.

One of the ships that will almost certainly be a part of the fleet will be a reproduction of the *Mayflower*. The ship dubbed *Mayflower 2000* will set sail from Portsmouth, England, to the New World in the spring of 1999 with a crew of about twenty, and ten or fifteen passengers. The voyage will take an estimated sixty-six days.

Sydney, Australia, probably has the jump on other world cities for a year 2000 celebration because it will be the site of the XXVIII (28th) Olympics. The Sydney Summer Games are expected to attract more than ten thousand athletes from 171 nations. The Olympics are always a huge event worldwide. The millennial year will make them even more so.

Though the calendar dates for the year 2000 are accepted by most nations, the numbering of the years is based on the Christian calendar—2000 years since the birth of Christ. Therefore it is not surprising that there will be large-scale millennial events in the Holy Land. That section of the world is now inhabited primarily by Jews and Muslims, but tourism officials are expecting anywhere from three to four million visitors to the region during the millennial period. Special events are being hosted in Bethlehem, Nazareth, and Jerusalem from 1999 to 2001. There is talk of a papal visit or perhaps a live concert by the Irish rock band U2.

While the Israeli Ministry of Tourism is planning to spend hundreds of millions of dollars to give Nazareth a face lift and improve the facilities in Jerusalem, little has yet been done to promote another Holy Land site with great millennial potential. It is a desolate ruin called Megiddo, thirty-five miles outside of the Israeli city of Haifa. That is the place where many believe that the end will begin.

Megiddo's fame rests on one sentence in the

Book of Revelation. After describing the end of days and the final battle between the forces of good and the forces of evil that will herald the second coming, Revelation says: "And they assembled them in the place called in the Hebrew language Armageddon." This is a corruption of the Hebrew word *har,* or mount, Megiddo.

The choice of Megiddo as the site for the cosmic showdown is no accident. It has now been deserted for some five centuries but in biblical times it was the site of many important battles. It is the place where the pharaoh Thutmose III defeated the Canaanites in the fifteenth century B.C., in what is the first documented battle between organized armies in history. It is where the biblical king Josiah was slain in the seventh century B.C., and it is where many fundamentalist Christians believe World War III will begin with the Arabs and Israelis, then involving all the other major powers in the world.

The ruins aren't much to look at right now. But Amy Docker Marcus, Mideast correspondent for the *Wall Street Journal*, writes: "From the top of the mountain, one feels the power of the notion of Armageddon continues to exert . . . In the fading afternoon light, the air is cold and the rising winds sound menacing as they howl through the stone ruins. The sky darkens to purple, and for a brief moment it's easy to imagine the sprawling valley below as history's ultimate battleground."

Archaeologists excavating the site are hoping that it can be developed into a major tourist attraction. Meditation areas are being built atop the mountain overlooking the Jezreel Valley. There is a possibility that high-tech computer screens will be located throughout the area, providing computer-generated images of what the city of Megiddo once looked like.

The Vatican has declared the year 2000 a Holy Year. Millions of visitors are expected to come to Rome to celebrate the Great Jubilee of the Incarnation of Christ between Christmas 1999 and January 1, 2000. There will be other observances and celebrations in Rome during the year.

Christians throughout the world, but particularly in the United States, are planning a March for Jesus on June 10, 2000. They hope to have over thirty million people in 2000 cities worldwide participating in the event.

Hanover, Germany, will be hosting what they call the bimillennial World's Fair in 2000.

There is going to be a Millennium Exhibition in Greenwich, England, starting in late 1999, though details of the exhibition have been hard to come by. The exhibition, called the "Millennium Experience," will be located on the North Greenwich Peninsula, about three miles from the city of Greenwich. The centerpiece will be a gigantic dome-like structure (the largest dome in the world), but no one seems to know exactly what it will contain. The one-billion-dollar proj-

The final moments of 1953 at the Chateau Madrid restaurant. *(AP/Wide World)*

ect has become very controversial in Great Britain.

The exhibition is supposed to celebrate time itself, and Greenwich is just about the best place in the world to do that, for in a sense it is the place where time begins. Greenwich is the location of the Old Royal Observatory and it contains the prime meridian mark from which all countries have measured longitude since 1884. Zone time based on the Greenwich meridian is recognized almost everywhere in the world.

A lot of people are going to look at the year 2000 as a time for a new age, a new beginning or

Visitors from Ohio celebrating in Times Square on New Year's Eve, 1988. *(AP/Wide World)*

a renewal of past commitments to make the world a better place. The environmental movement certainly feels that way. The year 2000 will also be the 30th anniversary of Earth Day, the main holiday of the environmental movement, and sponsors are planning the largest Earth Day ever, with over 300 million people participating in some way.

And this just scratches the surface.

All in all it's going to be a very interesting year.

CHAPTER 3

The Calculations of Denis the Little

The coming millennium is unique because it is the first time in human history that there has been a general agreement on dates and on the passing from one millennium to another.

People from different parts of the world may disagree over the significance of the date—but pretty nearly everyone agrees on the calendar. And the year 2000 marks the transition from one calendar millennium to another.

For most of human history people couldn't even agree on how long a year was supposed to be or when the year began. Certainly nobody thought in terms of decades, centuries, or millennia.

If you had asked a peasant living in Europe during the early Middle Ages what year it was he or she might have told you that it was the eleventh year of the reign of King So-and-So. And when did the year begin? To that he could have replied, on Easter, which was the first Sunday after the full moon following the spring equinox. More likely he would have just blinked at you in confusion and then said something like "planting time," or "harvest time."

Our medieval peasant may have had some thoughts about the Millennium (with a capital M), but they wouldn't have had much to do with the calendar.

It wasn't that dates weren't important to people in the Middle Ages. From the earliest times humans have been virtually obsessed by the passage of time. There were some obvious and practical reasons for this. The farmer had to know when his crops could safely be planted; the herdsman had to know when his flocks should be moved to safer pastures before the coming of the winter storms. The ancient Egyptians kept track of the time when the Nile River would flood and renew the fertility of their fields. Very early in human history the passage of time was marked by religious observations. Keeping track of time was generally in the hands of the priests or other religious figures of a community. They recorded the phases of the moon, the positions of the stars, and the level of the river.

At first glance the calendar looks easy enough. It is divided into days, months, and years—and these units appear to correspond to real events. The day is governed by the rotation of the earth on its axis, the month by the orbiting of the moon around the earth, and the year by the earth's orbit of the sun. Of course in ancient times people didn't know anything about orbiting or rotation, but everyone could see and experience the effects—the change from light to darkness, the regular appearance and disappearance of the moon, and the change of seasons. As far as we can tell people didn't begin trying to construct formal calendars until about five thousand years ago.

The problem for calendarmakers is that these events do not fit neatly together. For example, the lunar month is 29.53959 days and the solar year is 365.242199 days. (Actually it's even more complicated than that. The earth's rate of rotation is gradually slowing down, so that nine hundred million years ago days were only 18 hours long and there were more than 450 days in a year—but we don't need to worry about that here.)

Casual observations about the sun, the moon, and the seasons served well enough when people didn't know how to write and thus couldn't keep long-term records. But after people started trying to construct calendars, the differences began to show up. The result was that throughout most of human history people have used a wide variety of calendars, most of which were not very accurate, and which did not correspond with one another. The ancient Egyptians actually wound up using three different calendars, none of which were really accurate.

The Babylonians relied entirely on the moon. There were twelve lunar months, each beginning the day after a new moon was first observed by the priests. But since a lunar month is only a little over twenty-nine days, in a few years such a calendar will fall behind the actual progression of the seasons. So the priests stuck in an extra month every once in a while to make up the difference. But they didn't seem to have any regular system for adding the month, so it is not possible to reconcile the ancient Babylonian calendar with our modern one.

The ancient Greeks also used a lunar calendar, but they made it even *more* confusing. The Greeks were a notoriously independent people, and each local area had its own calendar controlled by local authorities. At times there were a hundred or more different local calendars in Greece, and they were all different.

The Romans were more organized. They had a big empire to run, and it was more important for everyone to agree on what year and day it was. At first the Roman year was 354 days and the priests would add an extra month whenever they thought it was necessary.

Not everyone needed an elaborate calendar. The native American tribes of North America, for example, counted the passage of time in moons and seasons but did not give years numbers and did not even have names for specific days.

The Mayans of Central America, however, had an extremely complex calendar. In fact, some people consider the Mayan calendar one of the most accurate up to modern times.

An interpretation of the Mayan calendar recently caused some excitement among the millennial-minded. Somebody figured out that according to the Mayan calendar, the end of the fourth creation of the cosmos, or the end of the world, will occur on December 23, 2012. The fourth creation started on August 13, 3114 B.C.

But what the alarmists didn't realize is that according to Mayan texts, the universal order will be reinforced, not destroyed, on the crucial date. The Mayan calendar actually advances well into the 50th century. According to University of Texas Mayan expert Linda Schele, "The ancient Maya would be celebrating it if they were here to see it."

There is much about the ancient Mayan calendar that still remains unknown and mysterious. Scholars do not know what they based their calculations on, or why. But it is clear that they did not regard December 23, 2012, as a doomsday date.

The Aztecs of Mexico used a calendar that was similar to that of the Maya. The Incas of Peru also had a calendar, but they had no written language, so we really don't know much about it.

Like the Mayans, the Aztecs of Mexico had a complex calendar that we still do not fully understand. *(Corbis-Bettmann)*

The ancient Chinese may have had the most accurate calendar in the world for many centuries. Chinese civilization is old and established. Their records go back a long way, and they had the best astronomical observations to boot.

When does the calendar begin? The Chinese began numbering years over six thousand years ago. The Hebrew calendar is dated from the beginning of the earth—October 6, 3761 B.C., according to tradition. Muslims use an Islamic calendar which is computed from a significant moment in the life of the Prophet Muhammad, July 15, 622 A.D., when he began the hegira, his flight from Mecca to Medina.

So why, amid all this diversity and all this confusion, is everybody getting so excited about the year 2000?

That buildup to the year 2000 really began in the sixth century A.D., though at the time there wasn't any sixth century A.D. The pope asked a monk named Dionysus Exiguus (translated that means Denis the Short, but it sounds more impressive in Latin) to calculate the date for Easter. Easter is the most important date in the Christian calendar, but it can occur any time between March 22 and April 25. It falls on the first Sunday after the full moon that appears on or nearest to the vernal, or spring, equinox—one of the two days in the year when day and night are exactly the same length. And there was a good deal of dispute about that. As you can imagine, fixing the date for Easter was no easy task. While doing this the monk calculated the year of Christ's birth and suggested that the years be numbered consecutively from that point to signify the Christian era and be designated A.D. for Anno Domini, or year of the Lord. Later scholars found that Denis was wrong about the date, and that Christ's birth took place from three to six years earlier than he had believed, but that has never had much effect on the development of the calendar.

The suggestion about numbering the years consecutively seemed a good one to Church authorities. It was practical. It set the Christian era off from what had come before. And this type of numbering was familiar. Years were traditionally referred to as the third or fifth year of a particular monarch. The system was gradually adopted in Christian countries over the next few hundred years.

But there was yet another problem. When did the year begin? That date was pretty much governed by local tradition. December 25 was a popular day for the New Year. So were March 1 and March 25. In some places the now familiar January 1 was used. In Athens, Greece, the year began in midsummer when new officials took office. In the non-Christian world the confusion multiplied. For Jews the New Year comes in

September and the Islamic calendar begins in July.

Up until the sixteenth century the Christian world was still operating under the calendar established during the time of Julius Caesar, but that calendar contained errors. The errors were small enough, but over time they accumulated and created problems. By the middle of the fifteenth century the vernal equinox was falling on March 10 instead of March 21. That upset the religious calendar, causing Easter to be celebrated too late in the year. At the Council of Trent, a gathering of the leaders of the Roman Catholic Church, a decree was passed authorizing the pope to correct the calendar.

That took a long time. Most of the calculations were done by the Jesuit astronomer Christopher Clavius. It wasn't until 1582 that Pope Gregory XIII issued a papal decree establishing what is now known as the Gregorian calendar. In order to correct past calendar errors, the day after Thursday, October 4, became Friday, October 15. January 1 was established as the beginning of the year. A few other more minor adjustments were made, and the result was an extremely accurate calendar, where the difference between the solar year and the calendar year is less than half a minute.

Is that the end of the story? Unfortunately no. Catholic countries adopted the Gregorian calendar almost immediately. But non-Catholic countries were far less enthusiastic. The American colonies did not begin using the calendar until 1752. It was called the New Style calendar. Russia didn't adopt the Gregorian calendar until after the Russian Revolution, in 1918. Greece waited even longer.

Today practically all the world's nations use the Gregorian calendar, at least for official purposes. Religious activities may still be guided by other, older calendars.

As you can see from this rather brief survey of the tangled and devious history of the calendar it is a purely human invention, a matter of convenience with no real cosmic or religious significance.

Why then is the millennium—the year 2000—such a big deal?

This is the first time in human history that practically everyone in the world recognizes the same calendar and the same date for the start of the year. And that's important. If we all didn't at least acknowledge the same calendar, modern high-speed transportation and communication would be in a state of chaos. Unlike our ancestors, we are not only aware of the calendar, we are ruled by it. If you place a long-distance call from New York to Hong Kong, it is helpful to know what time it is in Hong Kong. But what if you had to figure out what day and year it was as well because Hong Kong used a different calendar? You can see how confusing that would become.

Then there is the decimal system, counting by tens. There is still resistance to that in places like the United States where we measure by inches and feet rather than centimeters and meters, which are standard throughout most of the rest of the world. But generally ten and multiples of ten are the basis for our counting. Calendar years are measured by the decimal system—decades, centuries, and millennia.

In a 1992 *Time* magazine article Lance Morrow wrote: "The millennial date is an arbitrary mark on the calendar . . . The celebrated 2000, a triple tumbling of naughts, gets some of its status from humanity's fascination with zeros—the so-called tyranny of tens that makes a neat right-angled architecture of accumulated years, time sawed off into stackable solidities like children's blocks . . . The millennium is essentially an event of the imagination."

So on New Year's Eve 1999, while we are waiting for the world's odometer to tick over to the nice round number of 2000, it is going to be the first time in history that everyone will agree on the numbers of the millennium. The whole world's attention will be focused on that date. And we will all celebrate together.

And that really is a big deal.

CHAPTER 4

2000 or 2001?

Sit down and discuss the millennium with a group of people and you will almost always find someone who wants to argue about the date.

"The next millennium," he or she will say, "doesn't really begin until the year 2001."

Actually there's a lot of support for that point of view. The *World Almanac* says that the 21st century doesn't begin until January 1, 2001. The *Encyclopaedia Britannica* agrees; so does *Webster's Third International Dictionary* and so apparently do the Royal Greenwich Observatory and the U.S. Naval Observatory.

The science fiction writer Arthur C. Clarke certainly believed that the next millennium begins in 2001. He wrote a book called *The Sentinel,* which in 1968 was made into the film *2001: A Space Odyssey,* one of the most famous and influential science fiction films of all time. Clarke always insisted that 2001 was the beginning of the third millennium. In 1997 he followed up his first book with *3001*—that, in his view, is when the fourth millennium begins.

This isn't the first time that an argument like this has come up. A century ago Pope Leo XIII, Czar Nicholas II, President Charles William Eliot of Harvard, and *The New York Times* all agreed that the 20th century would begin with the year 1901.

There were a few who disagreed and thought the 20th century should start in the year 1900. One of the dissenters was Kaiser Wilhelm of Germany.

A debate over the date raged for months in the letters columns of the *Times*. In an editorial on December 8, 1899, *Times* editors pronounced themselves "much disturbed" by news the Kaiser had declared that the new century was about to begin. A few days later, the editors said, the Kaiser "must stand in solitary grandeur as the only man of any prominence who cannot count up to one hundred."

In still another editorial the editors insisted that it was "Beyond question, '1899' means the one thousand eight hundred and ninety-ninth year of the Christian era, and the next to last year of the nineteenth century."

The popular magazine *Literary Digest,* in its final issue of 1899, came down solidly for 1901. "If there was a year 0," the magazine asked,

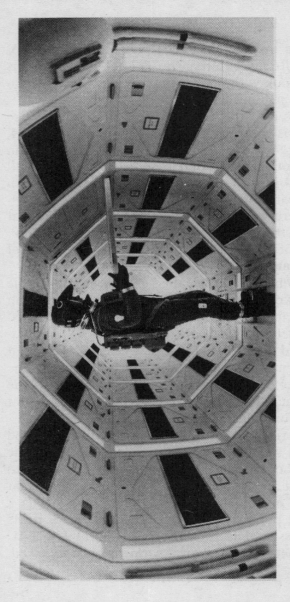

Scene from the famous science fiction film *2001: A Space Odyssey*, written by Arthur C. Clarke, who always insisted that the next millennium begins in 2001. *(Corbis-Bettmann)*

"why not a century 000. Perhaps there are only 399 society leaders in the 400! Perhaps we should begin counting our ages one year later, making us all a year younger!"

The article concluded with one troubling note, that in a hundred years it will all be forgotten, and some "'letter to the editor' will start the whole whirl going again."

Well, the "whole whirl" is certainly going again. But it wasn't a letter to any editor that started it. The current controversy is far bigger than anything that happened in 1899. Because this isn't just the mundane, more-or-less everyday end of a century. It is the end of a millennium. When does the old one end and a new begin? What about the missing year 0? Practically every article on the coming millennial celebrations mentions the 2001 controversy.

Journalist Richard E. Mooney agrees with the 2001 date for the millennium:

Putting it simply, for the 20th century to end with 1999, the first century would have had to end with 99 and, to make it 100 years, it would have begun with the year zero. But there was no year zero.

Indeed, the keepers of the calendar in ancient Rome did not even have a numeral for zero. There was no dispute about the end of the first century, because people had no idea that another century was about to begin. Centuries as we count them were unknown.

That's true enough, as far as it goes. But as lawyer and science writer Lee Loevinger has pointed out, the whole argument is completely pointless. There was no year zero. But there was no year one either, nor was there a year 99.

The current number of years didn't begin until sometime in the sixth century when that obscure monk Dionysus, or Denis the Short, calculated the time of Christ's birth and then suggested that years thereafter be numbered consecutively to signify the Christian era. That suggestion was generally welcomed by Christian scholars, but it was only adopted slowly over the next five hundred years or so.

Later research has indicated that the birth of Christ actually took place some three to six years earlier than Dionysus had calculated. So strictly speaking the third millennium has already begun. We are not going to celebrate the millennium too early as the die-hard 2001ers insist, but too late!

We don't really know whether the people of Europe a thousand years ago worried about whether the second millennium was going to begin in 1000 or 1001. Many of them probably didn't worry about it at all because they hadn't yet adopted the system of numbering years.

Loevinger believes that those who thought

about the matter at all "probably regarded the year 1000 as the beginning of a new century and a new millennium. The transition from a three-digit to a four-digit designation of a year surely would have suggested such a view."

But even if the Europeans of a millennium ago didn't think this way—and we really have no idea what they thought—Loevinger insists "It is reasonable to regard the year 1000 as the beginning of the tenth century and the second Christian millennium, the year 1900 as the beginning of the twentieth century, and the year 2000 as beginning the twenty-first century and the new millennium."

In the controversy over when the twentieth century began Neal H. Ewing offered a practical reason in a letter to the editor of the *Times* on July 20, 1899.

"The central figures are the symbol, and only the symbol of the centuries . . . The initial figure 18 [remember now that he was writing in 1899] is time's standard which the earth carries while it makes 100 trips around the sun. Then a new standard 19 is put up. Shall we wait now a whole year for 1901 at the behest of those who calculate by counting balls on an abacus?"

Michael Barkun, of Syracuse University's Maxwell School of Communications, offers another down-to-earth reason for assuming that the year 2000 is the time to celebrate the millennium.

He calls it "the unconscious tyranny that the decimal system exercises over our mind," our quasi-magical assumption "that round numbers have a certain significance."

The core of the argument about when the millennium begins isn't really about historical accuracy or the development of the calendar. It's about numbers. The year 2000 is a nice round number, an impressive number; 2001 is just another year.

You can probably still make reservations for New Year's Eve 2001 at the Rainbow Room and the Savoy—and Times Square will not be nearly as crowded then.

But it just won't be the same, no matter what the *Encyclopaedia Britannica* and the Greenwich Royal Observatory say. The real celebration for the new millennium will begin on December 31, 1999. That's what most people think—and this time most people are right!

CHAPTER 5

Where Will the Millennium Begin?

The new millennium will not begin simultaneously all over the world. The world is divided into twenty-four different time zones. So when they are popping the champagne corks and wishing one another Happy New Millennium in Sydney, Australia, people in New York will still have more than twelve hours to make final preparations for their party, and in Los Angeles they will have even longer to get ready.

Officially the day, the year, the century, and the millennium begin at the international date line. The international date line, established 114 years ago, is an imaginary line that runs jaggedly from pole to pole mostly through the Pacific Ocean. East of the line it is one day earlier than it is to the west. The international date line roughly, but only roughly, parallels the imaginary line marking 180 degrees longitude on the map.

The line was deliberately placed in the sparsely populated Pacific to avoid major land masses and minimize confusion. It's bad enough if the time in a place just a few miles away is an hour earlier or later—if it is a different day, that's much worse. The line bulges in some places to allow certain island groups to have the same day.

Normally, unless one is on a trans-Pacific flight or a round-the-world voyage, the international date line is of no great importance for the average person. It is not like a border between hostile countries. The international date line was intentionally designed to cause as little disruption and confusion as possible.

But with preparations for the millennium celebration, the international date line has suddenly become the object of international interest and controversy. Every day begins at this imaginary line. The third millennium will also begin there. With the immense worldwide interest in the millennium, the exact spot where it begins will be the object of a great deal of attention and its inhabitants will probably make a lot of money. For that reason there is a real fight to be the first place in the world to usher in the new millennium. Sure the location where the millennium begins is completely arbitrary, but so is the date itself. But it is also symbolic, and as a powerful symbol it cannot and will not be ignored.

The date line was deliberately designed not to touch any large land masses. Cruise ships and chartered flights will be right on the line when the new millennium dawns for what is being advertised as the ultimate millennial thrill. However, the exact bit of land where the millennium begins is what the controversy is all about. That's where the television cameras will be, and the tourists as well.

The main candidates are the South Pacific islands around New Zealand and Australia. They are all in the same time zone, so technically, as far as the clock and calendar are concerned, the millennium will start on all of these islands at the same time. But the more relevant question is where daybreak will be seen first. Which spot will be the first of the first? The difference is only a matter of minutes—but it is enough to separate winners from losers in the millennial record-book sweepstakes.

Probably the best claim, or at least a very good claim, can be made for New Zealand's Chatham Islands (pronounced *chaddum*). These tiny and sparsely inhabited islands are about five hundred miles east of New Zealand. Because of their distance from the mainland Chatham Islands residents have traditionally set their clocks forty-five minutes earlier than the New Zealanders.

But to the north, the tiny nation of Kiribati (pronounced *KIH-rah-bahss*) has put in its bid. The nation was once known as the Gilbert Islands. This string of thirty-six mostly uninhabited islands is best known for its president's decision to move the international date line.

According to President Teburoro Tito of Kiribati, this is not just a last-minute attempt to cash in on the millennium excitement. Before he changed it, the traditional date line cut right through the country. Today did not mean the same thing from one part of Kiribati to another. During a presidential campaign in 1995 Tito promised to move the date line to the east, off the 180-degree line, so that it goes around Kiribati and it is the same day in the entire country.

At the time no one paid any attention to the sharp new zigzag in the date line. And then people began thinking of the coming millennium—and they began paying very close attention.

"We're working hard to make this an eye-catching event," says President Tito. "We want the world to see Kiribati. We want to put Kiribati on the map." Well, Kiribati already was on the map; what the president did to the date line changed the map.

President Tito insists that he wasn't even thinking of the upcoming millennium celebrations when he promised to put his whole nation on one side of the line. "I was thinking of unifying the country," he said. "Later I realized I had accidentally made a good decision."

The result is that the Line Islands in the far east of Kiribati went from being one of the last in the world to see each new day to being among the first. The Line Islands are two hours ahead of the Kiribati capital, Tarawa, and an hour ahead of countries like Tonga, which sits very close to the international date line.

Kiribati's rivals for millennium business cried foul. But who were they going to complain to? There isn't any recognized international agency or rule to prevent a country from moving the line if it wishes.

The Royal Observatory in England, which devised the international system of longitude and timekeeping in the first place, has said that Kiribati was within its rights to make the change.

"There seems to be no legal reason why any country cannot declare itself to be in whatever time zone it likes, and it would be possible for any other island group further to the east of the Line Islands to declare itself to be keeping the same date," the Observatory said in a statement.

"This would obviously generate an absurd squabble, but if the financial return is sufficient and the tourists are gullible enough, it may happen."

So as things stand right now, clocks on Kiribati's Line Islands strike midnight at least an hour before clocks anywhere else on the globe.

Tourist officials on Kiribati are hoping to bring cruise ships to Caroline Island, an uninhabited speck that is the easternmost island of Kiribati, but the focus of the activities is to be Christmas Island, which has a population of 3,500.

The Royal Observatory in Greenwich, England, where the system of international timekeeping was first devised. *(UPI/Corbis-Bettmann)*

It is still not certain how successful this unilateral redrawing of the date line is going to be in the race for the millennial dollar. Other South Pacific islands are ready to try their own gimmicks. The island of Tonga, which is very close to the 180-degree date line, has been threatening to go on Daylight Savings Time, which would make it an hour earlier.

So the traveler who wants to be right on the spot where the new millennium first begins will have plenty of places to choose from. To a certain extent the world will decide where the millennium begins by where the world's television crews decide to set up their cameras. The most important factor may not be where the international date line is but where CNN is. The vast, vast majority of the world's people will experience the dawn of the new millennium on television rather than by visiting the international date line.

But for those who have the money and time to actually be at the place, many choices will be made on the basis of convenience. Greeting the year 2000 will be, first and foremost, a big party. While waiting for the moment to arrive, and in the hours and days after it passes, what will people do on the South Pacific islands? For those going to Kiribati the answer to that question is, not much. It is certainly off the beaten track. In fact, it is one of the least visited places in the entire world. On average all of Kiribati gets about four thousand visitors a year. Hawaii gets that many visitors in a few hours.

There are a few modest hotels scattered around the islands, and there isn't enough money around to build many new tourist facilities in the next two years. The little nation couldn't even handle a huge influx of millennial celebrants. So while Kiribati may gain some publicity and some visitors as a result of its fiddling with the international date line, its rivals in the South Pacific are not too worried.

Norris McWhirter, editor of the authoritative *Guinness Book of Records,* points out that New

Zealand's Antipodes Islands and Antarctica's Adelie Coast are probably the two points of land closest to the generally recognized date line. But these spots are so remote they make Kiribati look like Times Square. They may attract a small number of hearty souls, a very small number of hearty souls.

The island of Tonga, which is not exactly on the date line, but is close, has been making preparations to take advantage of the millennial boom for years.

"Tonga is going to make this a big celebration," Simote Poulivaai, secretary of the Tonga Tourist Association, told *The New York Times.* "We believe this will be the beginning and Tonga will move on from there and tourism will become much bigger."

Tonga's prime hotel, the International Date Line Hotel, has been fully booked for the last week of 1999 for well over a year, and several new hotels in Tonga are being planned to accommodate the expected (and hoped for) boom in tourism.

New Zealand is the best known place of any size to greet the morning. The town of Gisborne, a farming community of about 30,000, is the New Zealand community closest to the international date line. It is planning a major celebration with chartered flights bringing in millennial partygoers from all over the world.

"We're the first to see the sun, and we like to brag about it," said Trudi Roe, the secretary of the Gisborne Chamber of Commerce. "We're working madly to get organized, but everybody's trying to pinch this from under our noses."

The Chatham Islands, where the first rays of sunlight of the new millennium will become visible about 5:06 A.M., still appear to have the best and most authentic claim to be the first. Yet the islands seem less enthusiastic than many of their rivals to host the big party. Tourist resources on the islands are limited; there is only one modest-sized hotel and some smaller facilities, and there is no millennial building boom. It's not a tourist area and does not intend to become one.

Access to the islands is limited. A boat is probably the best way to get there. There is a single air strip, and the one commercial flight a day from mainland New Zealand is made by an Air Chatham turboprop plane that seats forty.

The Chatham Islands were invaded by the media—mostly the Japanese media—in 1989 to broadcast the arrival of a new decade. The islanders didn't like the experience, and that was nothing compared to what's bound to happen in 1999.

A variety of companies have been bidding to produce the first party of the new millennium on the islands. But according to Patrick Smith, who is the mayor of the only township on the islands, "We don't want the money taken off the islands." There is still a good deal of haggling going on over how the proceeds of any festivities will be split.

More importantly, Smith says, if the eyes of the entire world are going to be on the Chatham Islands, at least briefly, he wants them to welcome the new millennium with dignity. To mark the occasion, he would like to do something simple and symbolic, like releasing a dove. "We want to send a clean message to the rest of the world," he says. "In the year 2000 friends and families from all over will return to the Chatham Islands. Our people will come home. To me, that's the heart of the whole matter—it should be more of a family celebration."

CHAPTER 6

The Millennium and the Apocalypse

By strict dictionary definition a millennium is a period of a thousand years. That's easy. But the Millennium, with a capital M, is something different and far more complicated. It is a concept with a long and tangled history.

The only place in the Bible where a thousand-year period is prominently mentioned is in that most obscure and difficult and heavily interpreted part of the Bible, the Book of Revelation. In other parts of the Bible the significance of a specific time period is clearly downplayed with phrases like, "With the Lord one day is as a thousand years, and a thousand years as one day." Many scholars believe that the use of the word millennium should not be taken literally, but simply means a long period of time. Biblical literalists, however, insist that a millennium is a thousand years.

According to the most widely accepted biblical interpretations, the Millennium is a thousand-year period of peace on earth that will be granted after Christ returns. But others have interpreted the biblical references to mean that first there will be the worldwide triumph of Christianity and a thousand-year period of peace, which will prepare the way for Christ's return.

This second interpretation was adopted by increasingly optimistic eighteenth- and nineteenth-century clerics. They saw missionary work and other good works as a way to help bring about the Millennium.

But this doctrine was never really accepted by a large percentage of Christians. They believed that there was little that weak and sinful man could do to truly reform the world, and that peace on earth could only be prompted by the return of Christ. The Second Coming would mean Judgment Day, Armageddon (the site of the final battle between good and evil), the Apocalypse (an imminent cosmic catastrophe), and the end of the world as we know it. The Millennium would not be something built slowly through conversions and other good works—it would be a cataclysmic event that would occur suddenly and soon.

So in the popular view the Millennium is a very good thing that will be preceded by a series of very bad things including the cataclysmic battle between good and evil or between God and Satan.

In Christianity there has always been a powerful undercurrent of belief that this cataclysmic event was going to happen soon. St. Paul himself gave this vivid picture of the future:

> The Lord himself will descend from heaven with a cry of command, with the archangel's call, and with the sound of the trumpet of God. The dead in Christ will rise first; then we who remain alive shall be caught up together with them in the clouds to meet the Lord in the air, and we shall always be with the Lord.
>
> (I Thessalonians 4:16)

Note that Paul speaks of "we who remain alive." That makes it sound as if the event were going to take place in his lifetime, or the lifetimes of most of those who heard him. In his epistle to the Romans Paul says, "Now is our salvation nearer than we believed," and "The night is far spent, the day is at hand" (Romans 13:11–12). Examples like this are numerous in the New Testament.

In Christianity there is no doubt that Christ will return and the world will be transformed— the question is when. Even Paul, who clearly believed in the early return of Christ, had to counsel converts that it might not take place as soon as they wished. And later Church Fathers energetically tried to suppress movements based on a belief in an immediate Second Coming. They laid great stress on the biblical passage, "Of that day or that hour no one knows, not even the angels in heaven, nor the Son, but only the Father" (Mark 13:32).

There is absolutely nothing in the Bible to support a belief that Judgment Day will be January 1, 2000—or any other specific date. Most of the prophetic sections of the Bible talk about various signs like earthquakes and wars that will be seen before the final moment—not of specific times or dates.

The most striking and memorable image of the Apocalypse is that of the four horsemen described in the Book of Revelation. The meaning of the first of the horsemen, seated on a white horse, is unclear. Some think that this horseman is supposed to be a symbol of the returning Christ, others disagree. But there is little doubt about the meaning of the other three horsemen.

The rider on the red horse is war, the rider on the black horse is famine, the rider on the pale horse is death, probably in the form of plague or pestilence. Thus three powerful signs of the end of the world are great wars, great famines, and great epidemics.

The Four Horsemen of the Apocalypse as envisioned by the early-sixteenth-century German artist Albrecht Dürer. *(Corbis-Bettmann)*

The lack of biblical evidence for the exact time when the world is to end has not stopped people from trying to set a date anyway. Over the last two millennia, there have been hundreds of groups, large and small, that have insisted that they knew when the world would end. Usually such ideas had the greatest impact among people who were poor and powerless. They lived in misery and looked around and saw injustice and cruelty everywhere. They saw a world hopelessly sunk in sin and corruption, without any possibility that it could rescue itself. The only possible cure they saw for all their personal troubles, and for the troubles of the world, was a cataclysmic end followed by a new beginning.

Such movements are generally called millenarian because they are based on a belief in an imminent Second Coming and the start of the Millennium—the thousand-year period of peace, justice, and prosperity here on earth. The good (usually the people who hold such a belief) will be rewarded and the wicked (just about everyone else) will be punished.

An early millenarian movement was Montanism, which began in the second century. The movement was started by a newly baptized Christian named Montanus, who went into trances and uttered prophecies. He was soon joined by two women, the prophetesses Priscilla and Maximilla, and the three gathered a large following among the Christians of Asia Minor.

The Montanists expected the heavenly city of Jerusalem to descend from the skies at a place called Ardabau. This was to be the signal for the Second Coming.

The civil wars that ripped through the Roman world at the end of the second century were viewed by Montanists as sure signs that the end was near. In A.D. 198 there was a widespread report that numerous witnesses had actually seen a walled city in the sky over Judea. It had been seen on forty consecutive mornings. This vision was probably the result of a mirage, and it was in the wrong place anyway, but to the Montanists it could only be the heavenly city descending. Still, the end did not come.

Montanism, which for years had been a powerful alternative to orthodox Christianity, went into decline because it could not adapt to a world which stubbornly refused to end.

While Montanism itself disappeared, the millennial beliefs that brought it into existence in the first place did not. They resurfaced time after time throughout history, sometimes with tragic results.

In the year 1530 the German city of Munster was taken over by a religious sect known as the Anabaptists. This was an era of great religious turmoil, but the Anabaptists of Munster were extreme, even in an age of extremes. They believed the world was about to end because it had become hopelessly sinful and corrupt. In order to hasten the end, they were going to turn their city into New Jerusalem—the place where Christ would return to earth.

In order to "purify" their city they expelled all the Catholics and Lutherans and everyone else who disagreed with them. This provoked a powerful reaction throughout Germany, and Munster was attacked and surrounded by a large army led by the former bishop of Munster.

For the outnumbered Anabaptists the military situation was hopeless. But under the leadership of John of Lyden, who styled himself the Messiah of the Last Days, the Anabaptists of Munster held out. They were reduced to starvation and despair and finally overrun on June 24, 1535, and slaughtered, despite promises of safe conduct back to their homes if they surrendered.

A far happier group were the members of the Harmony Society, better known as Rappites. They were followers of Father George Rapp and they came to America from Germany in 1804.

The Rappites were millennialists who were convinced the end of the world was at hand. But they didn't just sit around waiting for the sky to open up. They worked hard but not too hard, for they thought work should be a pleasure not a punishment. All visitors to Rappite communities were struck by the cheerfulness and good health of the members.

"Father" George Rapp at the age of eighty.

Father Rapp, the likable and practical leader of the group, was utterly convinced that Christ would reappear in his lifetime. Father Rapp lived on and on in great good health and cheerfulness into his nineties. When he finally took sick he said: "If I did not know that the dear Lord meant I should present you all to Him, I should think my last moments come." Those were his final words.

CHAPTER 7

The Year 1000

What happened on New Year's Eve 999, some fifty generations ago and the last time a millennium rolled around?

There is a general impression that the world, at least the Christian world, was gripped in an "epidemic of terror." Many believed that the end of the world and Judgment Day were immediately at hand and that great and terrible things were about to happen.

Here is a famous description of the time written by the scholar Charles Mackay:

The scene of the last judgment was expected to be Jerusalem. In the year 999, the number of pilgrims proceeding eastward, to await the coming of the Lord in that city was so great that they were compared to a deserting army. Most of them sold their goods and possessions before they quitted Europe, and lived upon the proceeds in the Holy Land. Buildings of every sort were suffered to fall into ruins. It was thought useless to repair them, when the end of the world was so near. Many noble edifices were deliberately pulled down. Even churches, usually so well maintained, shared the general neglect. Knights, citizens, and serfs traveled eastwards in company, taking with them their wives and children, singing psalms as they went, and looking with fearful eyes upon the sky, which they expected each minute to open, to let the Son of God descend in his glory.

During the thousandth year the number of pilgrims increased. Most of them were smitten with terror as with a plague. Every phenomenon of nature filled them with alarm. A thunderstorm sent them all upon their knees in mid-march. It was the opinion that thunder was the voice of God announcing the day of judgment. Numbers expected the earth to open, and give up its dead at the sound. Every meteor in the sky seen at Jerusalem brought the whole Christian population into the streets to weep and pray. The pilgrims on the road were in the same alarm . . .

Fanatic preachers kept the flame of terror. Every shooting star furnished occasion for a sermon in which the sublimity of the approaching judgment was the principal topic.

This description, or descriptions very like it, have been repeated so many times that they have taken on an aura of one of those facts that "everybody knows." The story of the great end-of-the-world panic as the first millennium drew to an end is so dramatic and so logical that it just has to be true—but it probably isn't.

The first published account of the great panic of the year 1000 did not appear until some seven hundred years after the supposed event. There is absolutely no contemporary evidence that such a panic ever occurred. The story really got around during the eighteenth century, and was repeated by such eminent and influential persons as the French writer and philosopher Voltaire and the British historian Gibbon. The Middle Ages were viewed with great disfavor during the eighteenth century, and many writers were anxious to expose the superstitious and credulous nature of the people of the period. They seized upon the story of the great panic because it was useful for their cause and because they believed it. And why not? It sounded and still sounds plausible enough, particularly if one does not know a great deal about the Middle Ages.

Mackay wrote his account in about 1840. He was a pretty good scholar, but he was also very much a man of his time, enlightened and rational. He was eager to expose the foolishness and hysteria of an earlier time of superstition.

Historians Jacques Barzun and Henry F. Graff explained that a trained medieval scholar should be able to spot the story as a phony almost immediately.

"He [the historian] knew in the first place that the end of the world had been foretold so often that only the ignorant in the year 1000 would seriously believe a new rumor. Moreover, long before that year, it had become orthodox belief and teaching that if the end of the world were really to come no man would know the time in advance."

There were also other reasons for rejecting the story. Today the year 1000 sounds impressive and significant—as does the year 2000. But in the Middle Ages people still used Roman numerals. The year 1000 would have been the year M. That is, however, the reason that the word millennium is often capitalized. "For the Middle Ages," write Barzun and Graff, "no magic property would attach to 'the year M.' No doubt mystery and significance would then have been with 3s, 7s, 12s, and their multiples. For these were the sacred numbers of the Jews and the Christians had repeatedly used them for prophecy."

There was still no generally agreed upon calendar in Christian lands. When was the year supposed to begin? In some places the year began at

Christmas, in others at Easter. Other countries used the first of March or the first of September. "In such a state of things the world could obviously not end on schedule everywhere," the scholars comment.

Even though the Church had officially established the dating of calendar years beginning with the supposed year of the birth of Christ, that system was not universally accepted, even in Christian lands. And common folk may have generally been unaware that there even was supposed to be a millennium. They would still have thought of years the old way: the fifth year of the reign of King So-and-So. The people who lived at the end of the first millennium were not ruled by calendars as are we who live at the end of the second millennium.

There certainly was plenty of superstition in the world around the year 1000. It was a time that, for Europe at least, could be called the Dark Ages. Recordkeeping at the time ranged from poor to nonexistent. We have only the sketchiest notion of what was going on, how people acted, and what they believed. The world seems to have had its usual quota of war, hatred, and intrigue.

The idealistic Holy Roman Emperor (actually a German prince) Otto III came to Rome, where he installed his old tutor, the French cleric Gibert Aurillac, as Pope Sylvester II. The new pope was one of the most educated men in Europe and a reformer who dreamed of unifica-

A drawing taken from a medieval tapestry shows the excitement caused by an appearance of Halley's comet in 1066.

tion between the Western and Eastern branches of Christianity. He was so learned and so much of a reformer that his numerous enemies thought that he was a sorcerer and the Antichrist. The Romans who feared being ruled by a German emperor and a French pope were extremely unhappy. In 1002 Otto was poisoned by his Roman mistress. A year later Sylvester died under mysterious circumstances.

This was not a hopeful beginning to the second millennium, but it was business as usual in the politics of early medieval Europe.

Any major event—the sudden death of a powerful ruler, a war, a famine, an earthquake or bright comet, the emergence of a forceful and popular preacher—could, and often did, set off end-of-the-world panics during the Middle Ages. But these panics were local. They did not affect all Christian countries, much less non-Christians. News from distant lands was sketchy at best, and it arrived slowly if at all.

There can be absolutely no doubt that the end of the first millennium was nowhere near as big a deal as the end of the second millennium is going to be.

CHAPTER 8

Calculating the End

Most end-of-the-world scares are triggered by events—wars, famines, plagues, and the general feeling that the evil in the world has gotten completely out of control. But there have always been those who, despite the biblical admonition "that day or hour no one knows," have believed that they were able to figure out the exact day when the world would end. Despite the fact that there are no prophetic dates given in the Bible, some people are predicting a cataclysm at the start of the third millennium. Trying to calculate the exact date the world will come to an end is a task that has been tried time and again—and the calculations have always been wrong.

By the second century of the Christian era the most widely held belief among orthodox churchmen was that the world would end six thousand years after its creation. Since the world was then considered to be approximately fifty-seven hundred years old, it could not possibly end for another three hundred or so years. That seemed a comfortable length of time, no need to worry that Judgment Day was just around the corner. The date of creation was arrived at by adding up all the age references in the Old Testament. That was no easy task.

The second-century calculations, however, were rough and general. In 1650 Archbishop James Ussher of Ireland did a thorough job collecting Old Testament age references. From them he calculated that the earth had been created in the year 4004 B.C. This date was widely accepted in the English-speaking world and appeared in the margin of the first chapter of Genesis in many printed editions of the Bible. Some scholars refined Ussher's date even further by stating that Creation began at nine in the morning of October 24, 4004 B.C. Ussher, however, did not set a date on which the world was to end.

Others, however, have looked into the Scriptures and believed that they were able to calculate not only the beginning but the end. One of those was a simple and deeply religious upstate New York farmer named William Miller. And Miller's calculations were to set off what became one of the biggest and best documented end-of-the-world panics in history. The episode should serve as a lesson for all those predicting doomsday before January 1, 2000.

Miller was no fanatic and no fraud; he was a simple, sincere, and deeply religious man. In about the year 1816 he began the self-appointed task of studying the Bible thoroughly. After two years of study Miller was convinced that he understood the Scriptures and all their implications. Most significantly he believed that during the course of his studies he had discovered a vital, but hitherto unrevealed message; the end of the world was coming and it was coming very soon.

He wrote, "I was thus brought in 1818, at the close of my two years' study of the Scriptures, to the solemn conclusion that in about twenty-five years from that time all the affairs of our present state would be wound up."

The specific biblical passage that gave Miller his date for the end of the world occurs in the Book of Daniel 8:13: "And he said unto me, Unto two thousand and three hundred days; then shall the sanctuary be cleansed."

Miller interpreted the "days" as "years" in the prophecy. Since the prophecy itself was dated about 457 B.C., the end of the two thousand and three hundred "days" would come in about the year 1843. Given the many calendar changes that had taken place over nearly two thousand years Miller was unable to decide on the exact day or even the exact year this prophecy would be fulfilled. But he was convinced that the "sanctuary" would be "cleansed" around the year 1843.

The cleansing of the sanctuary could only

mean the purging of the earth by fire—in short, the end of the world, Judgment Day, the Second Advent or Second Coming of Christ was at hand. The trumpets would blow, the sky would roll back to reveal the heavenly host, the graves would give up their dead, and all the righteous would go to heaven and the sinners would be cast down to hell.

There was nothing particularly unusual about Miller's vision of Judgment Day. This vision was shared by all his churchgoing neighbors. Miller, however, was the only one who presumed to know the time when the great and awful event was to take place.

Instead of rushing out to proclaim the truth that he believed had been revealed to him, Miller became frightened by the thought that he might somehow be wrong. So he went back to his Bible and spent the next fourteen years checking and rechecking his proofs. He studied other prophetic references in the Bible. He made elaborate charts comparing the Hebrew and modern calendars. Everything he learned seemed to point to the same conclusion—the world was going to end around the year 1843.

It wasn't until 1831 that Miller began preaching his new doctrine. Starting in small local churches he moved on to larger and larger audiences. And he began picking up followers, including quite a number of clergymen, who then went on and spread Miller's doctrines to their

"Prophet" William Miller, whose calculations about the end of the world inspired a mass movement in the mid-nineteenth century.

own congregations. The term Millerite became common in upstate New York and rural New England. And it spread to the cities as well.

By 1842 the Millerites were holding huge camp meetings where thousands of people traveled by railroad, wagon, horseback, or on foot to hear Prophet Miller and other Millerite leaders preach and to engage in almost nonstop prayer sessions.

While Miller and his most devout followers needed only their Bibles to convince them of the absolute truth of their message, others looked elsewhere for signs of the approaching end. And they found them. Early in 1843 there was the sudden appearance of an exceptionally bright comet. Comets had always been regarded as omens of great and terrible events.

As the time neared, the ranks of the Millerites swelled, and the followers of William Miller became more and more excited. Facing the imminent end of the world you might imagine that the Millerites would be apprehensive or frightened. Far from it. They looked forward to it with great joy.

The Millerites were true millennialists. They despaired of this world and eagerly awaited its end and the dawn of a new world—the Millennium.

Miller hesitated to set an exact date for the world's end. At the beginning of 1843 he wrote: "I am fully convinced that sometime between March 21 of 1843 and March 21 of 1844, according to the Jewish mode of computation of time, Christ will come . . ."

A rumor swept the Millerite faithful that the date would be April 21, 1843. When April 21 passed without anything out of the ordinary happening the Millerite leaders quite properly pointed out that they had never endorsed any particular date, and the April 21 prediction had been made public mainly by their enemies.

When the calendar year of 1843 ended with

the world unchanged there was a more serious moment of disappointment. But the leaders pointed out that the critical period could be extended until March 21, 1844.

There may have been some defections at the end of 1843 but the months between January and March of 1844 actually saw an increase in Millerite activity and a flood of new converts to the ranks.

But when March 21, 1844 came and went without any fresh signs that the world was about to experience the Second Coming, that created a real crisis of faith. Miller himself wrote, "I confess my error and acknowledge my disappointment." But his faith was unshaken and he urged his followers "not to be drawn away from the truth." He was still absolutely convinced "the Lord is near, even at the door."

The Millerite movement was at a low ebb during the spring of 1844, but incredibly by the summer it began to grow again, and became more active and influential than ever.

One of Miller's followers, a man named Samuel Snow, did his own biblical calculations and determined that the critical date was October 22, 1844. After the March disappointment many in the movement fastened on the October 22 date. Miller himself hung back until October 6, when he declared that he was now fully committed to October 22.

So it was that Prophet Miller himself was

ultimately swept up by the movement he had begun, but could no longer control. The Millerite movement from top to bottom became fully committed to the prediction that the world would end on October 22, 1844.

Just exactly what the Millerites did or did not do to prepare for the great day is a matter of some controversy. There are lots of stories—still repeated today—that they donned white robes, called ascension robes, and trooped to hillsides or other high places to await the arrival of the Lord with much crying and shouting. There are even stories about Millerites who actually attempted to fly bodily to heaven by flapping their arms. And there are many tales of Miller's followers being carted off directly to insane asylums. Such tales are almost certainly exaggerations or downright fabrications.

Most Millerites stayed in their homes with their families or went to temples they had constructed to pray and sing with their fellow believers until the last moment. But when that deadline passed without anything at all happening, the blow was crushing.

One disappointed Millerite wrote: "Our fondest hopes and expectations were blasted, and such a spirit of weeping came over us as I never experienced before. It seemed that the loss of all earthly friends could have been no comparison. We wept, and wept till the day dawned.

"And now to turn again to the cares, perplexities and dangers of life, in full view of jeering and reviling unbelievers who scoffed as never before, was a terrible trial of faith and patience."

This final disappointment was too much. Miller once again confessed his error about the date and expressed his great surprise and disappointment. He again exhorted his followers to hold fast because the Second Coming could not be long delayed. But the movement was shattered and Miller himself died a sad and broken man in 1849.

But the end of the Millerite movement did not mean the destruction of the beliefs and emotions that had spawned it in the first place. Many of those influenced by Millerism went on to form the movement known as Adventism. An offspring of Adventism is the group Jehovah's Witnesses—one of the most vigorous and fastest growing religious movements in the world today.

While a belief that the Second Coming or Second Advent "is near, even at the door" is a cornerstone of the movement, modern Adventists fear repeating William Miller's mistake and hesitate to publicly set an exact date. Within the movement itself there have been rumors that the world would end in 1914 (not a bad prediction since that is when World War I began) and 1972. It is not unreasonable to assume that some will also fasten upon January 1, 2000.

CHAPTER 9

The Millennium Virus

When January 1, 2000, dawns, chances are the sky will not open up to reveal the four horsemen of the Apocalypse riding down upon us.

But many computers may begin acting as if they just had a personal brush with one of the four horsemen. Department stores may reject a credit card because the computer says the payments are one hundred years late. Telephone service may be cut off because of errors in date calculations. Automated teller machines will swallow bank cards thinking they have expired. People will be cut off of social security because the computer miscalculates their age. Airline flight schedules will be thrown into chaos and automatic elevator programs may crash, freezing elevators in high-rise buildings. VCRs won't automatically record TV shows because they won't know what year it is. That's pretty scary stuff.

The New York Times says that the story "at its most lurid sounds like the plot for a Hollywood disaster movie: At the stroke of midnight on Dec. 31, 1999, everything from telephones to air traffic control systems goes on the fritz. Mobs of people, unable to withdraw money from automated teller machines, storm bank buildings—only to find the vaults mysteriously open."

Not all of those things are going to happen. In fact most of them probably won't happen. January 1, 2000, won't be doomsday for computers as some alarmists have been freely predicting. But it will be a mess—it's already a mess, and it may ultimately cost billions of dollars to fix worldwide. This problem is called, among other things, the millennium bug, the millennium virus, or the millennium mess.

The problem really began in the 1960s and 70s when computers were beginning to make an impact on just about everything. At that time most computers were huge room-sized machines called mainframes. Despite their size these giant computers had only a tiny fraction of the memory that today's much smaller computers possess. In order to preserve memory space programmers limited dates to six digits, two each for the month, day, and year. Thus, years would be designated '67, '73, '81, '98, and so on. That was fine for the end of the twentieth century when the computer simply assumed that the first two digits of the year were 19. But what happens when the year comes up '00? Then the computer simply assumes that it's 1900, and that can create vast and sometimes incalculable problems. A lot of computer functions are built on programs that keep track of the passage of time.

This is not a problem that suddenly snuck up on people. Computer programmers knew what might happen twenty or thirty years ago when they were first installing the programs. They simply assumed that the programs wouldn't last to the end of the century, and if they did there would be some sort of technological quick fix developed to take care of the problem. But many of the early programs proved far more durable than anyone had imagined and are still around. There is no quick technological fix, no magic bullet on the horizon, and there is precious little time left to find one.

The owners of many computer systems are angry and bitter because the problem can potentially cause them great trouble and will certainly cost a lot of money to fix. The most common complaint is "They didn't tell us about this when they put the system in."

The problem is so bad, says George Luntz, president of a company that specializes in fixing the old systems, "that it has brought out all the conspiracy nuts, just like the Kennedy assassination. I assure you there was no conspiracy. We felt the useful life of these systems was five to ten years."

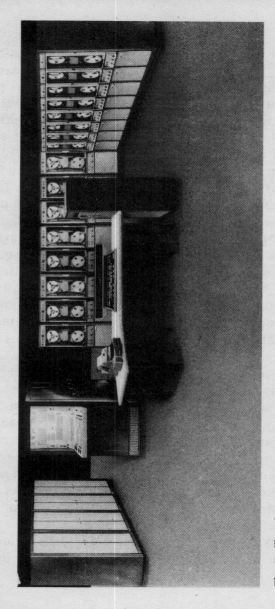

The "millennium virus" problem really began in the '60s and '70s, when most computers were huge machines that possessed only a fraction of the memory of today's small personal computers. (AP/Wide World)

After that people just procrastinated. Said Luntz, "The approach was in the great American tradition of, 'We'll fix it when we have to; we'll delay it until the final payment is due.' Well we've reached the final payment. This is the 30th year of a 30-year mortgage. They have to fix it—and fix it at once."

What many find so frustrating about the situation is that fixing the programs isn't going to make them work better. It will just allow them to keep on working. It's a lot like the boring task of resetting the clock on your VCR or microwave when Daylight Savings Time begins. When you are finished, your TV doesn't have any better shows, and your microwaved meal doesn't taste any better. In the case of the millennium bug an enormous amount of money, probably billions of dollars worldwide, is going to have to be spent for this resetting job.

One of the things that happened to create this mess is that the newer systems, which could easily accommodate a four-digit year, are still running on the old programs because it was easier and cheaper to import the old programs than to create and install entirely new software. So when the old program was put into the new computer, the millennium bug came with it. As a result no one is really sure how big the problem is or exactly where the glitches will appear.

To make matters worse the old programs are written in old computer languages that are no longer understood by young programmers trained to deal with the latest technology. It's a little bit like asking mechanics trained to work on jet engines to repair a steam engine. It can be done, but it would take a lot of re-training and time.

As a result there has been a sudden employment boom for older programmers, people who still understand the now obsolete mainframes and computer languages. These are people who may have installed the systems in the first place, but recently had been eased into retirement or otherwise pushed aside by younger programmers trained with the new hardware and software.

David Fowler, a former long-time employee of IBM who had been coaxed into early retirement years ago, has suddenly found himself in demand again.

"They were saying, 'The mainframe is dead,'" Fowler told *The Washington Post*. "They said they didn't need our talent." After a few years of playing golf and lounging around the Florida beaches Fowler now finds himself busier than ever fixing the year 2000 problem.

"They made me an offer I couldn't refuse," he said.

One group of formerly retired programmers printed up T-shirts reading: The Dinosaurs Are Back. The backs of the T-shirts read: And We Are Angry.

They are not only angry, they are getting rich. A

Daniel Cohen

programmer trained in thirty-year-old technology can now command higher fees than a recent college graduate skilled in the latest cutting-edge technology. That is not the way it was meant to be.

Fixing the problem is slow and tedious work. Every computer system and every program that contains dates must be opened up, examined, and changed to accommodate the change of millennium. This essentially means poring over printouts containing thousands of lines of code and checking for commands likely to affect dates. One of the most worrisome concerns is that even if one computer system is fixed to accommodate the century change it can easily be contaminated by dates imported from other computers that have not been fixed.

Here is the sort of thing that can happen. *USA Today* concentrated on the small city of North Platte, Nebraska:

At the police department, supervisor Mary Ann Agier noticed a problem with a program she uses to dispatch police file reports and track personnel. When she enters "00" for records that require expiration dates like local handgun permits a message pops up on the screen, "Date must not be in the past."

For now she often enters "99" when she has to enter 2000 or beyond. "But all of

78

these entries will eventually have to be fixed," she says. "Right now it's a minor inconvenience. But it's going to get worse."

Perhaps the problems caused by the millennial bug are most daunting at the United States Internal Revenue Service, the government agency that collects taxes. Even without this problem the IRS computer system has been widely criticized as being inefficient and out of date.

"We have an enormous problem which may be unprecedented in its complexity," Arthur A. Gross, the man in charge of the tax bureau's information systems, told *The New York Times*. "We can't get it wrong, because there won't be enough time to do it over."

The IRS has more than fifty different computer systems running 19,000 separate applications from more than 62 million lines of program code. And that is just the core business of processing 200 million tax returns and collecting $1.4 trillion in government revenue.

At the moment Gross estimates that it will cost $155 million to bring the systems up to date before the millennium ends, and he admits that the estimate may be low. Right now there are over seven hundred people working on the year 2000 conversion.

In addition to the core business the IRS uses an additional 30,000 programs on minicomputers and desktop machines for less critical functions. Gross admits that he has no idea of the scope or cost of converting them. "We don't know what we don't know." He said many of the systems will have to be discarded because it is too expensive to fix them.

At the Pentagon the situation is even worse. At congressional hearings in March of 1997 Emmett Paige, Jr., the Defense Department's top computer executive, testified that the Pentagon was about halfway through the process of assessing the problems. He said that they had already identified 560 computer systems that would have to be eliminated because they would be too expensive to make year-2000-compatible.

The current estimate, he said, was that it would cost about $1.1 billion, but that the costs would probably rise as the millennium drew near. Officials said that the estimated price did not include what it will cost to fix programs at the National Security Agency, the CIA, and other secret programs. The best that government officials could say was that they hope that they can get everything done that has to be done before the deadline.

Before the congressional hearings the problem of the millennium bug was discussed only within the community of computer professionals. After the publicity generated from the hearings, it became a problem that everyone was talking about. In an editorial published on March 22,

1997, *The Washington Post* admitted that there had been a "widespread and understandable impression that the whole thing is some kind of joke," but that the hearings had helped to dispel that impression. It's not a joke anymore.

The fear created by the looming specter of the millennium virus created something of a craze on Wall Street. Clearly a great deal of money was going to be spent correcting the problem, so any company that had even a remote claim to having a solution suddenly attracted a lot of attention. Stock prices on many of these companies suddenly shot up. A lot of people were betting a lot of money on the belief that they would make huge profits from the disaster.

The problem is that despite some promises, almost no one believes that there will be a magic-bullet solution; no single company is going to have the cure. Then in two years it's all over; either the problem has been fixed or it doesn't make any difference anymore.

Insurance companies have begun to provide year 2000 insurance against the damage caused by a company's failing to navigate the date change. But the insurance is expensive and it certainly doesn't fix the problem.

In its March 1997 editorial, *The Washington Post* tried to sound hopeful and upbeat. The newspaper concluded: "The existing world stock of computers may be too dumb to navigate the millennium, but some fraction of their hard-headed human overseers are sure to figure out a way to do just fine."

The *Post* is probably right. But if you want to tape the TV images of the millennial celebrators on New Year's Eve 1999, you had better test your VCR first, just to make sure that it can recognize the next millennium.

CHAPTER 10

The Future Isn't What It Used to Be

For the new millennium, prophets have predicted everything from a thousand years of peace to Armageddon.

On a somewhat less cosmic level, anniversary dates like the change of decades and change of centuries have traditionally brought out loads of predictions about what life will be like in the future.

There are plenty of predictions for the new millennium, but oddly, not as many as one might predict. Perhaps that is because past predictions have usually been so wildly, embarrassingly, and humorously wrong that the prophets have become a bit cautious. And some of them have completely fallen silent. The past has not been kind to those who like to predict the future.

In 1893 a group of prominent Americans offered their visions of what life would be like in one hundred years or so. A U.S. Senator predicted that "It will be as common for the citizen to call for his dirigible balloon as it now is to call for his buggy or his boots." Not many are calling for buggy and boots today, but even fewer are calling for balloons.

In 1908 aviation pioneer Wilbur Wright said: "I confess that in 1901 I said to my brother Orville that man would not fly for fifty years . . . Ever since, I have distrusted myself and avoided all predictions."

Wright's caution was not shared by Marshal Ferdinand Foch, French military strategist and World War I commander. Foch said, "Airplanes are interesting toys but of no military value."

Another memorable end-of-the-century prediction was made in 1899 by Charles H. Duell, U.S. commissioner of patents: "Everything that can be invented has been invented."

The head of the Western Union telegraph company turned down Alexander Graham Bell's offer to buy the fledgling phone company with these words: "What use could this company make of an electrical toy."

And then there was the prediction made by Darryl Zanuck, head of 20th Century Fox, in 1946: "Television won't be able to hold on to any market it captures after the first six months. People will soon get tired of staring at a plywood box every night."

By the way, 20th Century Fox will not be changing its name to 21st Century Fox.

In 1949 the magazine *Popular Mechanics* predicted that "Computers of the future may . . . perhaps weigh 1.5 tons."

As late as 1967 Lee De Forest, inventor of the radio, was sure that man would never reach the moon, "regardless of scientific advances." But then the great Scottish mathematician and physicist Lord Kelvin said "radio has no future."

More often than not the predictions for the year 2000 were too optimistic. In *USA Today,* reporter George Zoroya notes: "By the year 2000 . . . we were supposed to have factories without workers, offices without paper and a marketplace without cash. . . . AT&T predicted Americans would ham it up on picture phones from coast to coast. General Electric envisioned vaporizing household trash with lasers."

There were going to be electric cars and household robots, and nuclear power would supply cheap, clean, and safe energy for everyone. And through the miracle of antibiotics, infectious diseases were supposed to be a thing of the past. But then, DDT was supposed to take care of all insect pests.

Maybe Lee De Forest thought that we would never reach the moon. After we did, just about everyone predicted that there would be manned stations on the moon and manned voyages to Mars before the next millennium. Then priorities changed and the march to the planets stopped with one broken-down Russian space station and some tiny unmanned probes on Mars. In the space-age heyday of the 1960s, anyone who predicted that by the end of the millennium we would be going nowhere in space would have been denounced as a foolish pessimist.

In a series of World's Fairs and other exhibitions, the twentieth century was littered with displays of The World of the Future or The World of Tomorrow. One might reasonably expect that amid all the millennial hoopla there would be an explosion of Life in the 21st Century exhibits of one kind or another. But that really hasn't happened. That's because the future is now and tomorrow is today, so all of those earlier World of the Future exhibits have long since been dismantled or look hopelessly dated.

At the General Motors Futurama exhibit at the forward-looking 1964 New York World's Fair, planners envisioned colonies in Antarctica, on the ocean floor, and in the deserts. One futuristic device pictured was a nuclear road-building device about the size of a football field. This monster could plow through the rain forest cutting down trees with laser beams while laying asphalt. Put up an exhibit like that today and it would probably be attacked by angry visitors. Does anyone now want to see the Amazon jungle turned into a parking lot? That's not a vision for the next century—that's a nightmare.

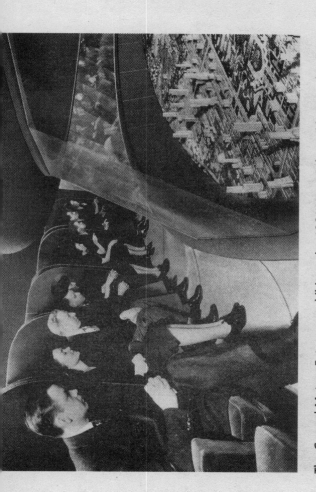

The General Motors Futurama exhibit at the 1964 New York World's Fair. (*Corbis-Bettmann*)

Housing of the Future, as seen in the New York World's Fair Futurama exhibit. *(AP/Wide World)*

Perhaps nowhere can the decline of this sort of technological prediction be seen more sharply than in the Walt Disney theme parks. The Disney parks have always been about more than cartoon characters. Since their beginning in the mid-1950s they have been relentlessly future oriented. The future on display was not just an entertainment future, or a science fiction future, but a "real" future. Many of the exhibits were designed to show the technology of tomorrow today. Walt Disney thought of himself as a middleman between industry and the public about communicating ideas of the future.

Take for example the Monsanto House of the Future that opened at Disneyland in California in 1957. It was designed by engineers at the Massachusetts Institute of Technology and built by the Monsanto Chemical Corporation. It was supposed to provide a realistic peek at how we would be living in the future—not the far distant future, but just a few decades into the future—in fact it was how we were supposed to be living in the 1980s.

It was a futuristic vision of a house mounted on a core rising some sixteen feet above the ground and made up almost entirely of curved fiberglass.

Inside, practically everything, even the furniture, was made of some kind of plastic. Disney officials were enthusiastic about this. "Hardly a natural material appears anywhere in the house," they boasted.

The Monsanto House of the Future, which opened at Disneyland in 1957, was a vision of the sort of home predicted to be common by the 1980s. (©*Disney Enterprises, Inc.*)

Appliances appeared at the push of a button; the height of the sink could be adjusted to fit the individual; there were wall-sized TV screens; and a climate control center that scented the air while regulating heat and humidity.

Does that sound like the house you live in? Do you know anyone who lives in a house like that? Of course you don't, because such houses don't exist. Some of the innovations, like the wall-sized TV screens, didn't turn out to be technologically feasible, though they may still be part of the future. Many of the other innovations failed simply because people didn't like them. The idea of living in an all-plastic house did not have great popular appeal. Actually the Monsanto House of the Future exhibit lasted only ten years before it became obsolete.

When Walt Disney first began to envision plans for his Florida development—Walt Disney World—he wanted more than a theme park. He wanted it to be the Experimental Prototype Community of Tomorrow (Epcot). He envisioned a futuristic-looking city built under a bubble of glass. It would be a place where families could live without having to hear garbage trucks and breathe fumes. It would not only be a place to live but a place to showcase and test all sorts of technological developments.

Walt Disney died long before he could fulfill his vision. And the Epcot that was finally built is really more of a trade fair attraction than a city.

To a large degree Epcot is a place where companies show off their latest products. It's high tech, to be sure, but it's not really a vision of the future.

The new Disney town, Celebration, is a far cry from Walt Disney's vision of a bubble-enclosed "city of the future." If anything, it looks like a city of the past—a slice of America before suburbs, highways, and strip malls. It is closer to the vision of America seen in the paintings of artist Norman Rockwell than to Walt Disney's vision of the future.

Celebration will fulfill Disney's dream to build a real community. The town is expected to house 20,000 residents. These people can look forward to living in a town that looks like Main Street in the Magic Kingdom, a fantasy version of nineteenth-century small-town America. The only furniture store in town specializes in reproductions of antiques, not futuristic plastic furniture. Of course, the town will make full use of modern technology—but it won't look modern or "futuristic." That's not what people want today.

The future has even caught up with the Disney theme park attractions in Tomorrowland. What had started out as the Rocket to the Moon adventure and became Mission to Mars in the 1970s has now been replaced by a new adventure featuring teleportation and an alien monster. It's called ExtraTERRORestrial Alien Encounter. The story line of the adventure is what happens when science goes wrong.

Despite a generous dose of imagination, the original Tomorrowland stuck fairly close to known science and technology. It presented an optimistic, perhaps over-optimistic, vision of the future—but it tried to be realistic. The newly made-over Tomorrowland has abandoned itself entirely to the realm of science fiction and science fantasy. It is the world of Jules Verne, H.G. Wells, *Star Trek, Star Wars,* and the old cartoon series *The Jetsons.* It has dropped any pretense of prediction of the real future. Even posters for Tomorrowland call it "The future that never was."

Professors and pundits of all kinds will undoubtedly look at these developments and draw all sorts of important conclusions. Maybe they will decide that the human race has lost its faith in the future of technology and has now turned inward to the imagination and to the past. From these conclusions they will then go on to predict what people of the next millennium will want and do. And the only safe prediction one can make is that all of these learned predictions will be wrong, just as they always have been.

CHAPTER 11

The Doomsayers

There have always been plenty of prophets of doom—people who insist that the world is coming to an end, and soon. Such prophets are bound to become more numerous as the year 2000 approaches.

Most doomsday prophecies are inspired by the Bible. But not all of them. There have been plenty of non-biblical prophets who predicted the end of the world—or appeared to.

Take the celebrated sixteenth-century English seeress Mother Shipton. Her most famous prophecy was a fifty-seven-line bit of doggerel that created a lot of excitement when it was first published. From the following extract it is easy to see why.

> Carriages without horses shall go,
> And accidents fill the world with woe . . .
> Around the world thoughts shall fly

In the twinkling of an eye . . .
Through the hills men shall ride
And no horse or ass by their side,
Under water men shall walk,
Shall ride, shall sleep, shall talk,
In the air men shall be seen
In white, in black, in green:
Iron on the water shall float,
As easily as a wooden boat . . .
Fire and water shall wonders do.
England shall at last admit a foe,
The world to an end shall come
In eighteen hundred and eighty-one.

Obviously the prophecy got the date for the end of the world wrong. But this prophecy was supposed to have first appeared in print in 1447! That would make the predictions about horseless carriages and iron ships pretty remarkable.

But there are problems with the prophecy. In the first place Mother Shipton is believed to have been born around 1488, about forty years after the prophecy was supposed to have been made. In fact, the first time this prophecy actually appeared in print was in 1862 in a book of Shiptonian prophecies edited by Charles Hindley. According to the editor it was a newly discovered prophecy of the famous seeress.

For the readers of the Hindley book the prophetic verses looked amazing and the predicting of the end of the world in nineteen years was something to worry about.

Mother Shipton, the English prophetess who was said to have predicted that the world would end in 1881.

The reality behind the prophecies, however, is quite unsensational and rather obvious. They are a forgery. Hindley admitted that he wrote the verse himself. He seems to have made a rather shrewd guess about the number of auto accidents that were to accompany the introduction of the horseless carriage; as for the rest of the predictions, they were not so remarkable when made by someone living in the middle of the nineteenth century. But when the book first came out, the end of the world prediction created quite a scare among its readers.

You might want to remember that phony

Mother Shipton prophecy when the supermarket tabloids and other publications begin hawking end of the world predictions as the year 2000 nears.

Unquestionably the most famous of all non-biblical prophets is the sixteenth-century Frenchman known as Nostradamus. The prophet's real name was Michel de Notredame (1503–66). His celebrated book called *Centuries,* first published in 1555, has interested and obsessed many people ever since.

Centuries is a collection of prophetic verses, each containing four lines (quatrains). These were arranged in ten books, each containing one hundred verses, called the *Centuries.* Actually, one of the books contains only forty-two verses, and the total number of verses is nine hundred forty-two rather than one thousand, as might be expected. Why the prophet did not produce a nice round number of verses is unknown.

The language in which the *Centuries* is written is extremely obscure. Nostradamus used a Latinized French that was archaic even in his day. He often employed puns and anagrams or simply made up words and phrases. He rarely put dates on his predictions and the *Centuries* are not in chronological order. A quatrain in the first Century might refer to an event that was to take place hundreds of years later, whereas a quatrain in a later Century might describe an event that was to occur within Nostradamus's own lifetime. He almost never used proper names. A ruler might be "the young lion" or "the Great King."

Nostradamus said that he made his prophecies deliberately obscure, because a clear prediction might get him into trouble. In the sixteenth century, predicting the death of the king was tantamount to treason, an offense that would quickly lead to a painful death.

The problem is that the prophecies are so obscure that they have to be heavily interpreted in order to make any sense out of them. The interpretations usually agree with what the interpreters already believed anyway. For example, during World War I French followers of Nostradamus who looked into the *Centuries* found a clear prediction of a French victory. Germans who interpreted Nostradamus's works saw predictions of a German victory. The French were right, but they also found predictions that the French monarchy would be restored and that the new French king would conquer Europe. That never happened. French followers of Nostradamus also said that Napoleon would conquer England and have a long and peaceful reign. That didn't happen either.

Interpreters of Nostradamus have been extremely clever at relating one of the prophet's quatrains to a historical event after that event has taken place. They have found predictions of the French Revolution, the rise of communism, Hitler and the Nazis, the development of nuclear weapons, the foundation of the state of Israel, Watergate, and the 1991 Gulf War—but only after these things had already happened. They have been far less successful using Nostradamus as a guide to the future. Followers of Nostradamus insist that while the interpretations may be wrong, the prophet himself is always right.

Nostradamus looms large in predictions for the year 2000. He doesn't actually come out and say that the world will end at the end of the second millennium; in fact many believe that his predictions stretch on until the year 3797. But it is clear that he predicted that something pretty important would happen before the end of this millennium.

In the year 1999 and seven months—
From the sky will come the great King of
 Terror
He will raise to life the great King of the
 Mongols
Before and after war reign, happily.

There are other references that apparently point to cataclysmic events at the end of the century, but this is the clearest, and one of the very rare prophecies in which Nostradamus actually uses a date.

The celebrated French prophet Nostradamus, who some believe predicted that the world will end around the year 2000.

But the prediction may not be as original as it seems. In Nostradamus's time it was assumed that the world was not very old, that it had begun sometime around 4004 B.C. Remember Bishop Ussher! A popular view at the time was that the world would last about six thousand years, which would bring us to around the year 2000. Thus, rather than making an original prediction, Nostradamus may simply have been building upon an already popular belief. Those who interpret the works of the French seer have had a variety of candidates for "the great King of Terror" and "the great King of the Mongols." There is no agreement as to the meaning of the rest of the quatrain, but it sounds important.

When you hear scare stories about how the great prophet Nostradamus predicted the end of the world at the end of the millennium, just remember that Napoleon didn't conquer England and a French king is not the ruler of Europe.

At the end of every year some of the supermarket tabloids and other publications print the predictions of modern prophets, psychics, astrologers, and the like. For the year 2000 this prediction business will certainly be bigger than ever.

The reason most of these prophets can get their predictions published is that people have short memories. They don't remember what the prophet predicted last year. If, by chance, he or she made an accurate prediction, the reader will hear about that. Wrong predictions are not mentioned.

But skeptics delight in collecting old predictions and comparing them to what actually happened. Often different prophets predict contradictory events. In the same year one prophet may predict a cure for AIDS while another insists that the AIDS epidemic will sweep the world like the black plague of the Middle Ages. Neither of these things has happened.

In past years prophets regularly predicted war with the Soviet Union, but virtually none of them predicted the fall of communism.

Prophets have also predicted that the lost continent of Atlantis would rise, that California would fall into the sea, that a UFO would land, and that Elvis would be found alive. Their predictions for the next millennium will almost certainly be just as reliable.

Since ancient times people have believed in omens and portents. Historically one of the most powerful omens was the appearance of a bright comet. Now that we know what comets are, they have been deprived of much of their danger and mystery. Still the appearance of a bright comet can provoke bizarre behavior in a few. The appearance of the Hale-Bopp comet, the brightest comet in a generation, in the spring of 1997 was one of the factors that triggered the mass suicide of members of the Heaven's Gate UFO cult.

The Heaven's Gate cultists did not believe that the comet was a sign of some approaching apocalypse; rather, they appeared to believe that the comet was being trailed by a giant spaceship—a UFO—that would pick them up and take them to "the next level." In order to reach this "next level" they had to leave their "vessels," or bod-

In 1997 Comet Hale-Bopp, the brightest comet in over a generation, seen here over the ancient stone circle Stonehenge, was viewed by some as a sign of the approaching end of the world. *(AP Photo/Alastair Grant)*

ies, behind. Tragically there will probably be similar events as we approach the millennial date.

Earthquakes are prominently mentioned in the Bible as a sign of the coming end. "And I beheld when he had opened the sixth seal, and lo, there was a great earthquake; and the sun became black as sackcloth of hair, and the moon became as blood" (Revelation 6:12). Any major and well-publicized earthquakes between now and the year 2000 will undoubtedly be pointed to as sure signs of the approaching cataclysm.

So will any major epidemics or plagues. A few years ago the AIDS epidemic was viewed as a sure sign that the world was in its final days. While AIDS is still a terrible disease it is no longer viewed as some sort of supernatural plague, and its power as a symbol of the apocalypse has diminished considerably.

"Great wars" are supposed to be another sign of the approaching end. Wars or any sort of political unrest, particularly in the Middle East, are always viewed with great interest by the apocalyptic minded. For much of the twentieth century the Middle East was believed to be the place where the final battle between the United States and the communist world would begin. With the collapse of communism this prediction has been rendered obsolete. Still, some saw the 1991 Gulf War as the opening act of the final battle. But bad as he is, Saddam Hussein of Iraq was never really powerful enough to be viewed as the evil ruler of the world who figures in so many end-of-the-world predictions.

In the United States today there are some who do not look to the Middle East for the start of the final war between good and evil—they think it's going to start right here. They believe that the federal government is about to sweep down on them and take away their freedom. They think that they will soon confront the power of a shadowy New World Order that is about to take over the United States. They are all ready to head for the hills to defend their lives, property, and freedom from this imagined threat. The approaching millennium is only going to make such people more nervous.

Orthodox Christianity has always condemned astrology, but this ancient practice has had a lot of believers, even in Christian lands. From time to time astrologers have looked at their charts and issued alarming predictions. As far back as the year 1179 the astrologer John of Toledo predicted a terrible catastrophe for the year 1186.

The reason for the astrologer's prediction was that he had calculated a rare conjunction of the planets. In a conjunction, the visible planets briefly appear to be at one spot in the sky. We now know that the planets only look as though they are in the same place. In reality they are millions of miles apart. But a lot of people took the prediction quite seriously and prepared, as best they could, for the disasters they were sure were going to strike. The astrologer was right about the conjunction, but wrong about the disaster. It was an ordinary year.

Even in modern times a conjunction of the planets is likely to set off a flurry of end-of-the-world rumors among the astrologically minded. A rare conjunction of five planets took place on February 5, 1962. In some parts of the world, where astrology still has a powerful grip on the public imagination, there were many end-of-the-world predictions. In the U.S. astrologers were more cautious. They just predicted that "something" would happen. Were the astrologers embarrassed when nothing unusual happened? Not in the slightest. They blandly asserted that "something" had indeed happened, but that we should not see the results of that "something" for many years to come. If, as some have hinted, the evil world ruler was born on that date he will be thirty-eight years old in 2000.

During the mid 1970s a good deal of attention was paid to what was called the "Jupiter Effect." A couple of scientists theorized that an alignment of the giant planet Jupiter with Earth and other planets might trigger massive earthquakes. If the theory had been correct the earthquakes would have taken place in 1982—but the theory wasn't correct.

In recent years there has been a lot of talk and worry about what has been called the Doomsday Rock—a gigantic meteorite, small asteroid, or comet—hitting the earth. The possibility that the earth would be hit by something large from space that would cause cataclysmic effects has always been recognized. But what made the possibility of such a cataclysm the subject of popular discussion was the discovery that just such an impact may have led to the extinction of the dinosaurs some 65 million years ago. If it happened to the dinosaurs, could it happen to us? Scientists have also become increasingly aware of the fact that there are a considerable number of fairly large objects out there in space that pass in the vicinity of the earth regularly. If one of them hit the earth it would be truly cataclysmic.

So we could be hit by the Doomsday Rock before the end of the millennium—but we probably won't be. This sort of collision is not a regular event in the earth's history. Of course, there are those who will mix a small amount of astronomical knowledge with a generous measure of apocalyptic fear and predict that the collision will take place soon. And there are others who will believe them.

No matter what instrument of destruction they envisioned and no matter what sources of information or inspiration they used, all the past doomsday prophets have had one thing in common—they have all been wrong.

When the millennial New Year's Eve party ends on the morning of January 1, 2000, the world will still be here. We will still have to pick up the paper cups and dirty dishes and sweep up the confetti—and get on with the next millennium.

CHAPTER 12

Marketing the Millennium

Imagine the T-shirt possibilities.

Surely everyone in America will have at least one T-shirt emblazoned with *I Survived the Millennium*.

Then there will be the embroidered millennium baseball caps with a big 2000 on them.

And there will be the mugs and the "collectors' edition" souvenir plates. How about the inevitable millennial Christmas ornaments, paperweights, and snow globes. Perhaps there will even be a millennial Barbie and Ken.

This is just the beginning.

Mazda has its Millenia sedan, Hilton its Millennium Hotel in New York. Farberware has its Millennium line of "never stick" sauté pans. The Millennium Mortgage Co. of Danville, California, is advertising loans for the 21st century.

La-Z-Boy offers Millennia office chairs. According to company executives "they have a very contemporary look."

Elizabeth Arden has its Millennium skin-care products. The product brochure raves, "In the present and future of every skin, there is a turning point—where it begins to appear tired, dry and older looking—but now there is an alternative. 'Millennium.'"

The Lever Bros. Co. is even using the millennium to sell soap with Lever 2000, a deodorant bar introduced in 1991. "It's a way of communicating a modern, up-to-date, innovative brand image," says a Lever spokesman.

In Wooster, Ohio, there is a Millennium Classic Bed-and-Breakfast. It's a white Victorian-style house, not exactly the image of the future. But the owners use the term millennium to evoke the image of the thousand-year period of peace, rather than the Apocalypse.

Starting next year a lot of items will be marked down to $19.99—Special End of the Millennium Sale. All the phone numbers ending in 2000 have almost certainly already been snapped up.

There is already a Fox television series *Millennium*. Created by Chris Carter, the man who gave us *The X-Files,* its view is a dark one. It seems the millennium will be characterized primarily by a dramatic increase in the number of really gruesome serial killings.

Many radio stations are already running spots called "millennium minute." They usually con-

Sydney, Australia, will host the Olympics in the year 2000. Souvenir koalas, kangaroos, and emus—part of the Australian Olympic Collection—are already being marketed. (Agence France Presse/Corbis-Bettmann)

tain a bit of past history. *Newsweek* has a page in every issue called "The Millennium Notebook" that serves as a forum to discuss how our lives will change in the future.

The ABC network and Hallmark Entertainment are trying to come up with a series about "what the year 2000 means." The network has contracted some of America's leading playwrights—John Guare, Larry Gelbart, David Mamet, Steve Martin, Elaine May, Terrence McNally, Arthur Miller, Neil Simon, Wendy Wasserstein, and August Wilson—to come up with a teleplay about that topic. The shows are scheduled to be broadcast during a single week of the November 1999 sweeps.

According to *Time* magazine, "At least two of the playwrights seem to be duly flummoxed by the nebulousness of the assignment. When asked what the year 2000 means, Gelbart, after some extemporizing, offers that it's a time for 'taking stock.' Wilson sees the millennium as offering humanity 'a clean slate,' although he is unsure what that might mean in practice."

One suspects that we will hear a lot about reunions and starting over, common enough themes in drama anyway. Every sitcom and every soap opera is going to have a lot of "taking stock" and "clean slate" episodes before the end of 1999.

The British Broadcasting Company (BBC) got a big jump on millennial planning. In 1989 they began work on what they call a "major, heavily funded" end-of-the-century documentary series.

There will be endless lists of the "greatest" men, women, events, and what have you, of the century or the millennium. And, of course, publishers are planning a flood of millennium books. This is one of them.

The great fear of those who are hoping to make a bundle out of the millennium is that the public will go on millennial overload. People will simply get tired of hearing about it.

Time's Bruce Handy complains that "the millennium already feels like a dud."

But hold on a moment, Bruce—sure we are going to be up to our eyeballs with millennium this and millennial that. By the middle of 1999 a lot of people are going to feel pretty fed up and there will be a lot of complaining that it's been overhyped and that it's not really a very important date anyway.

But today most events and holidays get too much hype. There are the Super Bowl, the Olympics, the presidential election, the big summer movie—even Christmas. Think about Christmas. Every year the Christmas season seems to start earlier. Now the Christmas catalogs begin showing up in the mailbox right after Labor Day. Everybody complains that Christmas is too commercialized, and by the second week in December all the new Christmas specials have been shown and we're on reruns. You begin to think

The illuminated ball that is lowered in Times Square every New Year's Eve will be the most familiar symbol of the millennial celebrations. A new and improved version of the traditional ball has been promised for the occasion. *(Reuters/Corbis-Bettmann)*

that if you hear "The Little Drummer Boy" just one more time you will begin screaming.

But by Christmas Eve the excitement is there, just as it always has been, and on Christmas morning you rush down to open those packages. Nobody talks about Christmas being too commercialized or over-hyped then.

It's the same with the millennium. There is going to be a lot of complaining, but in the end it's still going to be the biggest party the world has ever seen.

About the Author

Daniel Cohen is the author of more than 150 books for both young readers and adults, and he is the former managing editor of *Science Digest* magazine. His titles include *Ghostly Tales of Love and Revenge; Ghosts of the Deep; The Ghost of Elvis and Other Celebrity Spirits; The Ghosts of War; Gus the Bear, the Flying Cat, and the Lovesick Moose; Phantom Animals; Phone Call from a Ghost: Strange Tales from Modern America; Real Ghosts; The Restless Dead: Ghostly Tales from Around the World;* and *The World's Most Famous Ghosts,* all available from Minstrel Books, and *Hollywood Dinosaur,* available from Archway Paperbacks.

Mr. Cohen was born in Chicago and has a degree in journalism from the University of Illinois. He has lectured at colleges and universities throughout the country. Mr. Cohen lives with his wife in New Jersey.

SKATING FOR THE GOLD

MICHELLE KWAN & TARA LIPINSKI

WHO WILL BE THE NEXT OLYMPIC CHAMPION?

As the excitement of the 1998 Winter Olympics hits, all eyes are on two stunning figure skaters: Michelle Kwan and Tara Lipinski. Read all about these two skating superstars as each strives to win the next Olympic gold medal.

TWO SKATERS IN ONE BOOK!

PACKED WITH PHOTOS!

By Chip Lovitt

Available from Archway Paperbacks
Published by Pocket Books

1418-01

Meet The Man!
Meet Shaq!

SHAQUILLE

O'NEAL A Biography

REVISED

Shaquille O'Neal, the 7-foot-1 All-Star center for the Orlando Magic is dominating the world of big-time hoops with his size, quick smile and incredible basketball talent.

BILL GUTMAN

Available from Archway Paperbacks
Published by Pocket Books

1082-02

Have you ever wished for the complete guide to surviving your teenage years? At long last, here's your owner's manual—a book of instructions and insights into exactly how YOU operate.

Let's Talk About Me!

A Girl's Personal, Private, and Portable Instruction Book for life

Learn what makes boys so weird
Discover the hidden meanings in your doodles
Uncover the person you want to be
Get to know yourself better than anyone else
Laugh a little
Think a little
Grow a little

Top-secret quizzes, cool activities, and much more

Being a teenage girl
has never been so much fun!

FROM THE CREATORS OF
THE BESTSELLING CD-ROM!

An Archway Paperback
Published by Pocket Books

1433